THE H

Heist

SADDLEBACK
EDUCATIONAL PUBLISHING

3.0/1.0

T H E   H E I G H T S™

Blizzard	River
Camp	Sail
Crash	Score
Dam	Swamp
Dive	Tsunami
Heist	Twister
Jump	Wild
Neptune	

Original text by Ed Hansen
Adapted by Mary Kate Doman

SADDLEBACK
EDUCATIONAL PUBLISHING
www.sdlback.com

Copyright © 2012 by Saddleback Educational Publishing
All rights reserved. No part of this book may be reproduced in any form
or by any means, electronic or mechanical, including photocopying,
recording, scanning, or by any information storage and retrieval system,
without the written permission of the publisher. SADDLEBACK
EDUCATIONAL PUBLISHING and any associated logos are trademarks
and/or registered trademarks of Saddleback Educational Publishing.

ISBN-13: 978-1-61651-674-1
ISBN-10: 1-61651-674-7
eBook: 978-1-61247-378-9

Printed in Guangzhou, China
1211/CA21101853

16 15 14 13 12   1 2 3 4 5 6

Chapter 1

Jake Woods climbed into his truck. He headed to Springfield. The summer air was cool and fresh. But Jake knew it was going to get hot.

Jake had come a long way since his youth. As a teenager in Florida, he got into a lot of trouble. He'd made his living selling exotic swamp animals. It wasn't legal or right. But it was the only thing Jake knew how to do. Then he had some really bad luck.

Jake was in the wrong place at the wrong time. He was convicted of a crime he didn't commit. He went to prison. During work detail, he escaped into the Everglades.

Jake stole an airboat. It was the airboat the Silvas had rented for a tour that day. Pretending to be their tour guide, he took them through the swamp. The wild ride ended in a crash. Antonio Silva got pinned under the airboat.

But Jake didn't run. Risking being caught, he saved Antonio's life. It turned out to be the luckiest day of Jake's life. He and Rafael became friends. Rafael helped Jake get out of jail. The judge agreed. Jake was innocent.

Once Jake was free, Rafael got him a job. It was the second chance Jake Woods needed.

All that had happened years ago. Jake left Florida and moved north. He wanted to be closer to the Silvas. Now he was part of the family.

Jake had a small construction business. His company was hired to help drywall a five-story building. It would keep Jake and his crew busy for the next year.

The new building was called the Fargo Building. It was in downtown Springfield. The Springfield Bank was next door. It was a great location.

Jake drove his truck down the ramp into the basement. It was being used as a garage for the workers. Armed guards were watching. Jake thought it was strange. But he didn't ask why. He just went to work.

At noon everyone stopped for lunch. Jake sat with his foreman, Rob Torres.

"Rob, why does the first floor look bigger than the basement?" Jake asked.

"I never noticed," Rob answered. "Is it really bigger?"

"It looks bigger," Jake replied. "Maybe it's just an illusion."

Jake decided to measure the space. He walked the width of the first floor. It was 170 feet. Then he went to the basement. The guards looked at him. But Jake walked across the room anyway, counting his steps. It was only 160 feet. Jake knew something strange was going on.

Chapter 2

Jake wanted to know what was going on at the job site. He couldn't figure it out. So he went to the Silvas for help.

"Something weird is going on at the Fargo Building," Jake said.

"What do you mean?" Rafael responded.

"There are armed guards in the basement. But there's nothing down there. It's just an open space," Jake explained. "Also, the basement is smaller than the first floor. I can't explain it. It doesn't make sense."

Jake pulled out a blueprint of the building. He laid it on the table. Rafael looked it over. He shook his head.

"You're right," Rafael said. "This doesn't make sense."

"Can I look?" Antonio asked.

"Sure," Jake said. "Maybe you can help."

Antonio looked at the blueprints for a while.

"I think I figured it out!" Antonio shouted. "It's pretty crazy. But hear me out."

"Enough with the drama, Antonio. What's your theory?" Franco asked.

"Ten feet of space can't just disappear," Antonio said. "I bet someone built a fake wall in the basement. The Springfield Bank is right next door. A robber could tunnel into the bank and steal millions!"

Chapter 3

Rafael, Jake, and Franco were speechless. It was a crazy idea, but it made sense. It explained the missing ten feet and the guards.

"No way, Antonio," Franco said. "That's ridiculous!"

"But it would be a great plan," Jake said. "What if they tunneled into the bank on a Sunday? The bank would be closed. No guards would be on duty. They wouldn't know they'd been robbed until Monday."

At work on Monday, Jake paid attention to everything. A big truck was parked in the far corner of the basement. The words Dunn Electrical were painted on the side. That was strange. Electricians were not needed today.

Jake didn't want to draw attention to himself. So he asked Rob Torres to check out the truck. When Rob got too close, a security guard stopped him. He told Rob to go back upstairs.

"This is crazy," Jake thought. "Could Antonio be right?"

On Tuesday morning the truck was still in the basement. That was when Jake made a plan. It would change his life. Later that night, he was going to sneak into the Fargo Building. He wanted to check out the truck and the fake wall.

After midnight, Jake drove to the construction site. He parked a block away and walked to the Fargo Building. The basement was dark. It looked deserted. But Jake saw a small light inside the truck. Someone was sitting there. He was on the phone. It was the middle of the night. Nobody should be there.

As Jake got closer, he dropped to his hands and knees. He crawled around the outside of the truck.

There was a four-foot hole in the wall behind the truck.

"It's now or never," Jake thought. He climbed through the hole. It opened up into a wide room. Men were digging a tunnel.

"They don't even have to take the dirt out," Jake thought. "They can store it behind the fake wall. I've got to get out of here."

Jake turned to leave. But a man spotted him. He hit Jake over the head. Jake was out cold.

Chapter 4

No one had heard from Jake for two days. Rafael had called him over twenty times. He was worried. This was not like Jake. Something must be wrong.

Rafael, Franco, and Antonio went to the Fargo Building. He asked a guard where he could find Jake.

"His crew is on the first floor," said the guard.

Six men were working on the first floor. But Jake wasn't there. A man asked Rafael if he needed help.

"Yes," Rafael replied. "My name is Rafael Silva. I'm looking for Jake Woods."

"Oh, Mr. Silva," said the man. "Jake has talked a lot about you. I'm his foreman, Rob Torres."

"Hi, Rob," said Rafael. "Nice to meet you. These are my sons, Franco and Antonio. We're looking for Jake. Have you seen him?"

"No," Rob said. "I haven't seen him since Tuesday. He hasn't been at work the last two days."

"That doesn't sound like Jake. Did you report him missing?" Rafael asked.

"No, I didn't," Rob replied. "He's the boss. I thought something important must have come up."

"Here's my number. Please call me if you hear from him. But ask him to call me too. I'm worried about him."

Rafael, Franco, and Antonio went back to their car.

"What's going on, Dad?" Antonio asked. "Where's Jake?"

"I don't know," Rafael said. "But I'm going to find out. I'll call Chief Vega. Maybe he'll know what to do."

Rafael called the Rockdale Heights Police Department. An officer told Rafael the chief was camping. His cell phone didn't have reception in the woods. And he wouldn't be back until Monday. All Rafael could do was wait. He hoped Jake would turn up before then.

Rafael turned on the Monday morning news. He was shocked by what he heard.

"Over twenty-eight million dollars was stolen from a Springfield bank this weekend," the newscaster said. "The thieves built a tunnel from the Fargo Building. They entered the bank through a hole in the floor.

"Police believe this burglary took months to plan. This was not a one-person job. An arrest warrant has already been issued. Police think one of the Fargo Building construction workers was involved. Jake Woods is their prime suspect. He has not been seen since last week."

Jake needed help fast. Rafael needed to do something. So he called Chief Vega.

Chapter 5

Rafael told Chief Vega about Jake's discovery.

"Believe me," Rafael said. "Jake didn't do this. He's the one who thought something was wrong in the first place. He's being set up!"

"I'll call the Springfield Police Department," Chief Vega said. "I'll get their chief to meet with you. He needs to hear your story."

Chief Callas agreed to meet with them later that day. Rafael told him about Jake. He explained Jake's theory about the Fargo Building.

When Rafael finished, Chief Callas stared at him. He didn't look happy.

"Well, Mr. Silva," Chief Callas said. "I think Jake Woods did know about the tunnel. And I think that's because it was his idea. I bet he told you that story so you wouldn't suspect him."

Rafael started to respond. But the chief held up his hand to stop him.

"It's a done deal," said Chief Callas. "We have enough evidence to arrest Jake. You know he has a criminal record."

Again Rafael tried to respond. But the chief wouldn't let him.

"Woods would be a suspect even if he didn't have a record. His fingerprints are all over the tools in the tunnel. And he just purchased a plane ticket to Mexico. We even found plans for the tunnel in his house. He's thought about this for a long time."

Rafael couldn't believe what he was hearing. But he knew there was no point arguing. Chief Callas was convinced Jake was guilty. To him it was an open-and-shut case. Just then the phone rang.

Chapter 6

"We've arrested Jake," Chief Callas crowed. "I need to end our meeting, Mr. Silva. You know the way out."

Back at home, Rafael filled his family in on what happened.

"Jake's been arrested," Rafael said. "Springfield's Chief Callas thinks he's guilty. Jake's in a lot of trouble. He needs our help."

"Jake is like a member of the family," Ana said. "Tell us how we can help."

"We'll begin tomorrow morning. Franco and Antonio," Rafael said. "You two go see Rob Torres. See what he remembers about the guards. They had to be in on the burglary.

"Ana, you and Lilia call JJ Long. He's a private detective. I've known him forever. Ask him to find out everything he can about Victor Stone."

"Who's Victor Stone?" Ana asked.

"He's in charge of the whole Fargo Building job," Rafael said. "I've heard he's shady. He may be the guy behind the burglary."

"Sounds good," Ana said. "But all of you be careful."

"I'll hire a lawyer for Jake," Rafael said. "Then I'm going to go see him at the jail. We need to hear his side of the story. I also want to know where he's been the past five days."

"This is cool," Lilia exclaimed. "We're going to solve a crime!"

"Yeah," Franco added. "Let's hope that we don't mess up."

The next morning, the Silvas started their investigation. Rob Torres met with Franco and Antonio.

"We know Jake is innocent," Franco said. "We need your help to prove it."

"I thought that's what you wanted," said Rob. "One of the guards looked familiar to me. Then

I remembered he went to my high school. His name is Doug Harrington. He was a great football player. I can't believe I didn't recognize him before. Here's my high school directory. It has Doug's address in it. Maybe his family still lives there."

"That's very helpful," Antonio said.

"The truck parked in the garage had the words Dunn Electrical on it. That's all I can think of that may help you," Rob said. "I wish I could tell you more."

"No, you've helped us a lot," Franco said.

Chapter 7

Rafael met with his lawyer friend. He was one of the best criminal defense lawyers around. Rafael told him about Jake Woods. The lawyer took the case right away. They set up a meeting with Jake at the Springfield Police Station.

The pair got to the station at one o'clock. They waited for Jake in a small room.

Rafael hadn't seen Jake in over a week. He looked awful. Jake had lost at least five pounds. He hadn't shaved. And it looked like he hadn't slept in days.

Rafael introduced Jake to the lawyer. Jake thanked them both for coming.

"You're always getting me out of trouble," Jake said.

"Don't worry about that now," said Rafael. "Just tell us what happened."

"I'll tell you what I can," Jake said. "But everything is foggy. I think I was drugged."

"Do the best you can," his lawyer said. "Every bit of information is important."

Jake told them how he snuck into the Fargo Building. He told them about the hole in the wall. He told them about getting hit over the head.

"I woke up in a small room," Jake said. "My feet and hands were tied. But then they must have knocked me out again. The next thing I remember is the police picking me up. I don't even know how I got home. My head was killing me. I didn't even know the bank had been robbed until I was arrested. It's all a blur. I just can't remember!"

"That's okay, Jake. We believe you," his lawyer said. "It sounds like you were drugged and set up. Don't worry, we'll get you off."

31

That night the Silvas talked about what they'd found out. Ana had a report on Victor Stone. No one at the Fargo Building had seen him in weeks. JJ Long called Stone's office. It looked like he was involved. His assistant said he'd taken a leave of absence.

Rafael couldn't believe how much information Rob Torres had given Franco and Antonio. They could finally talk to a guard. If they could find him. It may be the break they needed.

"Doug Harrington is our best lead," Rafael said. "We'll check him out tomorrow."

Chapter 8

The directory Rob had given them
was from Westfield High School.
Westfield was about twenty-five
miles north of Springfield. It was
thirty-five miles away from the
Heights.

Rafael didn't think the locals
would help him find Harrington. So
he had a plan. He pretended to be a
reporter. He said he was writing a

story about former star athletes. He'd ask about Harrington's past. Then he'd find out what he was up to now.

Franco and Antonio wanted to go too. Rafael let them. But he made them wait in the car.

Rafael's first stop was the house Doug lived in during high school. It didn't take him long to find it. Rafael rang the doorbell. Nobody was home. It looked like no one had lived there for a long time.

A man next door was working on his car.

"No one has lived in the old Harrington house for a while," the man said.

"Oh," Rafael said. "Well maybe you can help me."

"What do you want?" the man growled.

"I'm looking for Doug Harrington," said Rafael.

"What do you want him for? Is he in trouble again?" the man asked.

"No. It's nothing like that," Rafael replied. "I'm writing a story on former star athletes. I wanted to get some information on Doug."

The man smiled.

"Oh, why didn't you say so? That boy was the best football player Westfield ever had. He played tight end. The kid had great hands. If the ball was near him, he caught it," the old man said.

"So I hear," Rafael responded. "Do you know where I can find him?

I'd like to take his picture for the magazine."

"He moved to Springfield. He's got a trailer north of town," the man responded. "I'll get the address for you."

Rafael thanked the man and went back to his car. Franco and Antonio asked Rafael if he got any information on Doug.

"Yes. I have his address in Springfield. We'll head over there now," Rafael said.

"What are we going to do when we get there?" Antonio asked.

"I'm not really sure yet," Rafael replied. "But we'll think of something."

They found Harrington's place right outside of town. Sitting on

about an acre was an old trailer.
There were also rusty cars and four
sheds. The place was a mess. It
looked like a junkyard. The driveway
was empty. It didn't look like Doug
was home.

"Let's check out the sheds,"
Franco said.

"Sounds good to me," said
Antonio. "What are we looking for?"

"Anything that can connect
Harrington to the Springfield Bank,"
Rafael said. "It seems safe enough.
Nobody's home. We'll each take a
different shed."

Antonio ran toward the biggest
shed. He opened the doors and
looked inside. The shed was filled
with trash. In the middle was a big

truck. The words Dunn Electrical were painted on the side.

The door to the shed slammed shut. Antonio turned around. A huge man was staring at him.

"Who are you?" the man yelled. "And what are you doing in here?"

Antonio froze. He tried to yell. Nothing came out. It was Doug Harrington! Antonio tried to run past him. But Doug reached out and grabbed Antonio by the neck.

Antonio couldn't breathe. Doug was strangling him! But right before Antonio passed out, the shed door flew open.

Rafael couldn't believe it. Doug was trying to kill his son. Rafael jumped on Doug's back. He hit him with all his strength. Rafael had caught Doug by surprise. Doug didn't have a chance.

The fight lasted less than two minutes. Franco was able to tie up Doug while Rafael called the police.

Once Antonio caught his breath, he showed Rafael and Franco the Dunn Electrical truck. It was the evidence they needed to tie Harrington to the burglary.

Chapter 9

Chief Callas stared at Rafael. He did not seem happy. But he smiled a little before he spoke.

"I don't like it when citizens try to act like cops," Chief Callas said. "But in this case, I have to say you did a good job. Tracking down Harrington and finding the truck was great detective work. But it was stupid."

"I know, Chief," said Rafael. "I should have called you first."

"Yes, you should have," the chief said. "You guys could have gotten hurt. If he'd had a gun, I don't want to think about what could have happened."

"You're right, Chief. I promise it will never happen again. But what about Jake Woods?" Rafael asked. "Are you going to let him go now?"

"Not yet," said Chief Callas. "I need to hear what Harrington has to say first. I'll keep Chief Vega up to date. I'll have him call you when Jake's getting out."

Rafael couldn't believe their luck. Not only did they find Doug

Harrington, they caught him too!
Pretty soon Jake would be free.

Doug Harrington was locked in
a tiny room. He was waiting to find
out what would happen to him. Chief
Callas came in. He sat down across
from Doug.

"Mr. Harrington, listen carefully
to what I have to say. I'm only going
to say it once," Chief Callas said. "We
know you were in on the burglary.
We have witnesses that saw you at
the scene. The truck that blocked the
fake wall was found on your property.
You're looking at fifteen years."

Doug Harrington stared at the
wall. He didn't say a word.

"But there may be a way out for you," said the chief. "We don't think you planned the job. And we know you didn't do it alone. What we really want is the top guy. We may be able to cut you a deal."

Doug Harrington finally looked at the chief. He seemed interested, but he still didn't talk.

"Tell me everything you know about the burglary," the chief continued. "And I'll recommend a reduced sentence."

"How long would I have to go to jail?" Doug asked.

"I'd say less than a year," Chief Callas said. "And you'd have to give your cut of the money back. Think about it. Fifteen years is a long time."

"You've got a deal, Chief Callas," Doug said.

All of the Silvas were excited. They couldn't wait to see Jake. When they got home, they found out Ana had more good news.

"JJ Long called an hour ago. He found out more about Victor Stone," Ana said. "Victor gambled a lot. He was in debt. He owed $250,000. Victor paid it off Monday. Then he just disappeared. No one has seen or heard from him since."

"Wow!" Rafael exclaimed. "That's very interesting. I bet he's somewhere spending his millions."

Chapter 10

Doug Harrington was nervous. He was in a room filled with police officers and tape recorders.

"You want to know who planned the bank job. But I don't know his name. No one did," Doug said. "I can only tell you who got me involved. His name is Kirk Blake. He's a small-time crook. He's the only person who knows who the top guy is."

"Well," Chief Callas replied. "Then tell us everything you know about the heist."

"Blake needed eight guys. He said we'd only work for ten days. Then we'd each get five-hundred thousand dollars. First we built the wall. It only took us one weekend to build it," Doug said. "Then we started digging the tunnel. We'd dig as much as we could every night. We kept the truck in the corner to hide the hole. My job was to guard it. I had to make sure no one came near."

"Did Jake Woods have any part in the burglary?" Chief Callas asked.

"No," Doug replied. "We found him looking around one night. It was Kirk Blake's idea to frame him."

"What happened after the burglary?" the chief continued.

"We put the money in the Dunn Electrical truck. Then we went to my shed. Kirk Blake paid us. Then he took the rest of the money. Blake told me to keep the truck. I haven't seen him since," Doug said.

Just then an officer walked into the room.

"Chief, I have some information you need to know," said the officer. "We just pulled a body out of the river. His ID says that his name is Kirk Blake."

Jake was released later that afternoon. Rafael picked him up. It was the second time Jake owed his freedom to Rafael.

Rafael told Chief Callas all about Victor Stone. The police believed that Victor planned the job and murdered Kirk Blake. They looked everywhere for him. But he was nowhere to be found. Victor Stone had disappeared with over twenty-five million dollars.

Six months later, Victor Stone was still on the run.

It was a snowy December morning in the Heights. The phone rang at the Silva house.

"Good morning, Rafael," a voice said.

"What's up, Chief?" said Rafael.

"I just wanted you to know that Victor Stone was caught yesterday," Chief Vega replied.

"That's great news, Chief," Rafael exclaimed.

"Yes," the chief continued. "He was living in Canada. He's on his way back to Springfield right now. They're charging him with burglary."

"What about the murder of Kirk Blake?" Rafael asked.

"Chief Callas wants to charge him. But they don't have enough evidence. They really need the murder weapon," said Chief Vega. "Should I recommend that the Silva family be put on the case?"

Both men laughed.

"No thanks!" Rafael exclaimed. "The Silvas are done with police work for a while."